FREDERICK WARNE

Published by the Penguin Group
London, New York, Australia, Canada, India, New Zealand, South Africa
First published by Frederick Warne 1998
3 5 7 9 10 8 6 4
Copyright © Eric Hill, 1998
Eric Hill has asserted his moral rights under the
Copyright, Designs and Patents Act of 1988
Planned and produced by Ventura Publishing Ltd
80 Strand, London WC2R 0RL
All rights reserved
ISBN 0 7232 8370 2
Printed and bound in Singapore by Tien Wah Press (Pte) Ltd

Spot's Bedtime Storybook

Eric Hill

FREDERICK WARNE

Contents

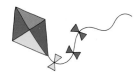

Spot's Windy Day

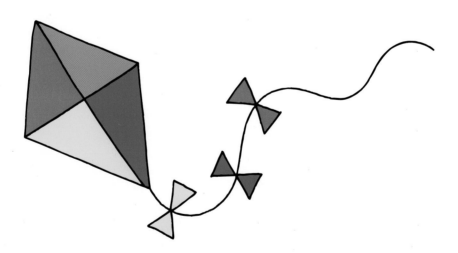

One windy day Spot went out to fly his kite.
"See you later, Mum," he called to Sally.
"Don't get blown away, Spot!" said Sally.

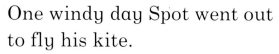

Spot ran up and down the field with his kite, trying to get the wind to lift it up into the air. Suddenly a strong gust caught the kite.
"Oh!" Spot cried. "Look how high it is!"

Then, "Oops!" said Spot. "How did that happen?" His kite had landed in a tree.
Spot looked up at it. "I can't reach up there," he said. "That's the end of flying my kite. Oh drat!"

Spot started to walk home. He was a little sad. Leaves were blowing all around him in the wind. Red, yellow, green and orange ones.

11

"I'll try and catch a leaf," he said. But it was harder than he thought. As soon as one came near him, the wind whisked it away again.
Spot looked up and saw something big and dark above him. It wasn't a leaf. "Ooh!" Spot said, reaching up. "What's that?"

It blew here and there. It came lower and lower—and *whoosh*—it landed right on Spot's head and covered his eyes.

Spot couldn't see anything.
But he heard a voice say, "Well, well,
there's my hat!"
Spot pulled on the sides of the hat and
someone pulled on the front. *Pop!* Off
came the hat and Spot found himself
looking up at Mr Kangaroo.

"Thank you, Spot. You saved my
best Sunday hat!"
"It was nothing," said Spot.
"I wish I could do something for you,
Spot!" said Mr Kangaroo.
"You can!" said Spot. "My kite is
stuck up in the tree. Can you
reach it?"

13

"Certainly," said Mr Kangaroo.
He jumped up and knocked the kite
down to the ground.
"Wow," said Spot. "I'm glad
your hat found me!"

Spot's kite once again
soared up in the sky.
"Thank you, Mr
Kangaroo!" shouted
Spot.
But Mr Kangaroo
couldn't hear. It was
too windy.

Spot's Surprise Parcel

"Spot, will you go and give this letter to Mr Bear the Postman for me, please? I can see him coming along the road now," said Sally.

"Yes, Mum," said Spot, taking the letter. He ran down the path.

When he reached the gate Mr Bear was just coming in with a big square parcel.

"Hello, Spot," he said.

"I have a parcel for you."

Spot took the parcel from Mr Bear. It was almost as big as he was. He couldn't wait to open it and see what was inside.

"Look, Mum. A parcel for me! Can I open it?"
"Did you give my letter to Mr Bear to post?" asked Sally.
"Oh sorry, Mum, I forgot," said Spot.
"Well, run and see if you can catch him and then you can open your parcel."

Spot ran down the path. His friend Steve was swinging on the gate.
"Hello, Steve. Did you see Mr Bear?"
"He's gone, Spot. Can you come and play?"
"First I have to post this for my mum. Then I have to open a parcel that just came for me. Then I'll come out and play."

Spot went to post the letter. But the letter-box was too high for him to reach.
"I need something to stand on," he thought. "I know!"

He ran back indoors and got his parcel. He carried it carefully all the way to the letter-box. He put it on the ground and climbed onto it. Now he was just high enough to reach the opening. He popped the letter in and carried his parcel back home.

"I've posted your letter, Mum. Can I open my parcel now?"
Sally helped Spot pull off the paper. Spot lifted the lid of the box and looked inside.
"What's in there, Spot?" asked Sally.

"It's a big ball!" shouted Spot.
"It's from Grandma and Grandpa," Sally told him.
"Can I take my new ball out to play with Steve?" asked Spot.
"Yes," said Sally. "And have fun."

Spot and Steve played with Spot's new ball all morning. It was really bouncy.
"I love my big round ball," said Spot.
"But I'm glad it came in a big square box so I could post Mum's letter! Catch, Steve!"

Spot's Lost Bone

"I've lost my bone," said Spot. "I've looked behind the chair and under the carpet. I can't find it anywhere, Mum."

"Maybe it's in your toy box," Sally told him.
Spot opened his toy box. It was full of toys, all the way to the top. Spot took them out one by one—cars, blocks, a train, a boat, a ball and his teddy bear.

Spot emptied his toy box but he didn't find his favourite bone.
"My bone's not here," he said.
"Maybe it's in a drawer," said Sam, Spot's dad.

"Don't forget to put your toys back," said Sally. "Or you might lose them too."
Spot put his toys back in the box.
Then he looked in the bottom drawer. It was full of books, crayons and games.

23

His bone wasn't in the bottom drawer
so Spot looked in the top drawer.
It was full of buttons and thread
and string. And stuff.
But no bone.

"I can't find my bone
anywhere," said Spot.
"Where can it be? I know,
I'll look in the cupboard
under the stairs."

The cupboard was full of brooms, baskets and buckets, and even a broken umbrella. Spot looked all the way to the back of the cupboard.
"Hey!" a voice squeaked at him.
"Oh!" said Spot, a little scared.
It was a tiny mouse.

"I've lost my bone," Spot told the mouse.
"Well, it's not in here," the mouse said.
"Maybe it's outside."
"The garden!" shouted Spot. "That's where it is! I remember now. Thanks, Mouse!"
And he ran outside.

Spot came back pulling the bone behind him, tied to a piece of string.

Sam laughed. "So you found your bone. Are you taking it for a walk?"

"No," said Spot. "I'm making sure that I don't ever lose my favourite bone again!"

Spot Follows His Nose

One morning Spot went out for a walk.
He stopped and sniffed. "What smells so nice?" he asked.
Spot went to the flowers in the garden. He sniffed.
"No. That's not what I can smell," he said.

His friend Helen came by on her bike.
"Hello, Spot. Why are you sniffing?"
"I can smell something really nice," Spot said,
"but I don't know what it is."

"Mr Kangaroo has just cut his grass," said Helen.
"Maybe that's what you can smell."
Spot ran across to Mr Kangaroo's house.

"Hey, Spot!" Mr Kangaroo shouted.
"What are you doing with my pile of grass?"
"I was only sniffing at it," said Spot.
"But it's not the smell I'm looking for."

Next door Tom was painting the fence in front of his house.
"I wonder if it's the paint I can smell?" said Spot.
He went up to the fence and sniffed.
"That smells awful!"

Tom laughed. "You've got
paint on your nose!"
Spot rubbed his nose.
"I have to go home now,"
he told Tom.

As Spot went up the path to his house, the smell got stronger. He ran inside.

Sally was polishing a table in the hall. Spot jumped up and sniffed at the table top.

"You've put your dirty paws all over my nice clean table!" cried Sally.

"I'm sorry, Mum," said Spot. "I've been smelling something nice all morning. But this isn't it."

"Why don't you look in the kitchen, Spot?" said Sally.
Spot ran to the kitchen. "That's the smell!" he shouted.
There on the table was a plate of hot cookies.

"I baked these for later," Sally told him. "But you can have one now." She smiled. "There's nothing wrong with your sense of smell, Spot!"
"No," Spot said. "And there's nothing wrong with my sense of taste either. Thanks for the cookies, Mum!"

Spot in the Snow

One morning Spot woke up and got a big surprise. Outside, everything was covered in snow.
"Mum, can I go out with my sledge?" Spot asked.
"Yes, but be sure to put on your hat and scarf," said Sally. "It's very cold outside."

"I don't need all that, Mum," said Spot, opening the door.
"Brrr! You're right, Mum. It *is* cold."
Spot put on his hat and scarf.

By the time Spot had pulled his sledge to the top of the hill he was feeling warm again.

He sat on his sledge and pushed himself off. *Whoosh!* Down he went to the bottom of the hill. "This is great!" he said.

Steve was skating on the pond.
"Yo-ho, Spot!" Steve called out.
"Do you want to try my skates?"

Skating looked easy when
Steve did it. But Spot
found it wasn't so easy
after all.

"Whoops!" said Spot. "I think I'll stick with my
sledge instead. Come and ride with me, Steve."
They climbed the hill, pulling the sledge together.
When they reached the top
they got on the sledge.
"Ready, steady . . . go!"

The sledge went much
faster with Spot and
Steve both on it.
"*Whee!* This is
fantastic!" shouted
Steve.
"Yes," cried Spot.
"Watch out for the . . .
Oh!"

The sledge hit a big pile of snow at the
bottom of the hill and came to a sudden stop.
Spot and Steve rolled out into the snow.
"It's a good thing that the snow is so soft,"
said Spot.
Then something not so soft knocked
Spot's hat down over his eyes.
"What's that?" Spot asked.

They heard giggling, and there was Helen,
laughing at them all covered in snow.
"It's a snowball," she called. "And here's
another!" And before he could move, a big,
squishy snowball hit Steve in the tummy.

"Here's one for you!" yelled Steve, throwing a snowball back.
"And another!" shouted Spot.
"Hey!" said Helen. "Two against one isn't fair.
Come and help me build a snowman. Look, I've
already started."

Helen had rolled a big snowball
for the snowman's body. Spot
helped her roll another one for
his head.
"Come and help us, Steve,"
called Spot.
"In a minute," said Steve.
"I'm busy."

Helen and Spot put the head on the body. They found two stones for the snowman's eyes and a piece of wood for his mouth.
"Look at our snowman, Steve," called Spot.
"And look at what I've made," said Steve.

Steve had made a "snowdog" on top of Spot's sledge. It looked a lot like Spot.
"That's great!" said Spot. "Why did you build it on my sledge?"
"So you could take it home, Spot."
"Mum will be surprised when two Spots come home," said Spot. "It's lucky she told me to wear my hat and scarf so she'll know which is me!"

Spot Finds a Key

Spot was playing in the garden. He saw something shining on the path. "What's that?" he said. "It's a key!"
"Perhaps it's a key to the garden shed?" said a bird.

"Let's see," said Spot. He tried to put the key in the lock of the garden shed but it was too small.

"Dad might know where this key comes from," said Spot.
"Here he is. I'll ask him."
But Sam was in a hurry.
"Sorry, Spot, I can't stop now. I'm looking for something."

"Oh well," said Spot, "I'll try indoors.
Perhaps it's the key to Mum's
jewellery box."

He tried to put the key in the lock of Sally's jewellery box but
it was too big.
"I'll ask Mum," said Spot. "Mum, do you know what . . ."
Sally didn't stop to listen. "Sorry, Spot, I must go and
help Dad. I'll be back in a minute."

"Perhaps it's the key to the desk,"
thought Spot.
He tried to put the key in the lock
of the desk.

The key was the right size but it
wouldn't turn.
"Nearly, but not quite," said Spot.
"This game is fun. Where else
shall I try? Perhaps it's the key
to the kitchen cupboard."

He put the key in the lock of the
kitchen cupboard. It was the right
size and it turned the lock, but it
didn't open the cupboard.
"Oh," said Spot, disappointed.
"What else can there be? Hello,
I wonder why Dad's left his
tool-box on the floor? Now that's
got a lock . . ."

Spot put the key in the lock of the tool-box.
"It's the right size . . . and it turns . . .
and it opens the tool-box!"

Just then Sally and Sam
came in. "Dad," said Spot,
"I've found the key of the
tool-box."
"Well done, Spot," said
Sally.
"That is clever," said Sam,
"because we didn't even
tell you what we were
looking for!"

Spot
in the
Woods

It was a beautiful sunny day.

"Come on, Spot. Let's go for a walk in the woods," said Sam.

"Oh yes," said Spot.

As they walked along, Spot looked around. "Are there any lions or tigers in the woods, Dad?" he asked.

"No, nothing like that," said Sam.

"Are there any elephants or bears?" Spot asked.

"No, Spot, nothing like that," Sam told him. "It's nice and quiet here in the woods."

It *was* quiet, but in some places it was dark too. Spot stopped walking and looked from side to side. He thought he saw something stripy through the leaves. Could it be a tiger?

No, it was just a tabby cat.
"Hello, Cat," said Spot. "Are there any tigers in these woods?"
"Oh yes," said the cat. "Lots and lots."

Spot walked on. He saw something golden and smooth in the shadows. Could it be a lion's coat?

It was a little fawn.
"Hello," said Spot. "Are there any lions in these woods?"
"Of course," said the fawn. "Tigers too."
"Oh!" said Spot. He walked on.

Spot could see something moving behind him.
Was it a bear? No, it was just a fox cub.
"Are there any bears here?" asked Spot.
"Of course there are," said the fox cub.
"Lions and tigers too."

Spot looked all around.
Was that grey patch by the log the end of an elephant's trunk? No, it was only a tiny grey mouse.
"Hello, Mouse. Have you seen any elephants round here today?"
"Oh yes, I play with them all the time," said the grey mouse.

Spot looked and listened more carefully than ever. Suddenly he heard the sound of something crashing through the bushes. It must be very large. Could it be an elephant? Or a tiger? Or a lion? Or a bear?

Phew, it was only Sam, coming back to look for Spot.

"Are you enjoying your walk, Spot?"

"Yes, Dad. But can we go home now?"

Sam was a little surprised. But still, it was nearly lunch-time.

On the way home, Spot stayed very close to Sam. He didn't see a lion or a tiger or an elephant or a bear. They were probably somewhere else in the woods. If they were there at all . . .

Spot Goes Splash!

It was raining when Spot woke up.
"Oh, dear," he thought. "I'll have to stay
indoors. I wonder what Steve and Helen are
doing today?"

"Breakfast is ready,"
Sally called from the
kitchen.
Spot loved breakfast. He
forgot all about the rain.

After he had finished eating, Spot looked outside again. "Oh, good," he said. "It's stopped raining. Can I go outside and play, Mum?"

"All right," Sally told him. "But don't get all wet and muddy. I've just cleaned the house before Grandma and Grandpa come to visit."

Spot went out into the garden.
The sun was beginning to shine.
Spot saw Steve looking up at
the sky.

"Do you see the rainbow, Spot?"
asked Steve.
"Yes!" said Spot. "It's so many
different colours."

Helen came along wearing a raincoat,
a big rain hat and shiny red rubber boots.
"It's stopped raining, Helen," said Spot.
"I know," said Helen.

"You don't need your raincoat
and hat and boots any more,"
Steve told her.
"Yes, I do," said Helen, smiling.
"Especially the boots. I need
them to walk through puddles.
Like this . . ." And she stamped
through a big puddle.
Splash!

"That looks like fun!" said Spot.
"Let's try it!" said Steve. And they splashed
through the puddles too, stamping and shouting.

"You two are silly," said Helen. "Now
your feet are all wet and muddy."
"We don't care," they said. "This
is great!"

"It's starting to rain again," said Helen. "I'm still nice and dry, and you two will have to go home."
"I suppose so," said Spot, having one last splash.

By the time he got home, Spot was very wet and very muddy.
Sally was not pleased.
"Get into the bath at once," she said.

"But it's not time to go to bed yet," said Spot.
"I know," said Sally, "but it's time for a bath."
So Spot got into the bath with
his boat and toy duck.

"This is fun, too," he thought.
"But after this I think I've had
enough water for one day."

Spot at the Fair

Grandma and Grandpa took Spot to the fair.
There was so much to see and do.
"What would you like to go on first, Spot?"
"I'd like to go on the merry-go-round," said
Spot. "Please."

Grandpa lifted Spot up
onto the horse.
"You too, Grandma and
Grandpa," said Spot.

"This is fun," Grandpa said. Grandma agreed. "Ooh, I can't remember when I last did this."

"What next, Spot?" asked Grandma.
Spot looked around. "I'd like to go on the helter-skelter," he said.

Spot came whizzing down.
"Wheee!"
"I'd like to go on that," said Grandpa.
"Me too," said Grandma.

Grandma came down the slide followed by Grandpa.
"This is great, Spot. What a time we're having!"
Spot laughed to see his grandparents having so much fun. Then he went on the helter-skelter again.

"Can I go on the bumper cars now?" Spot asked.
"I'll sit with you," said Grandma.
"I'll just watch," said Grandpa.

A loud buzz sounded and Spot pushed down on the
pedal. They were off.
"There's Helen and Tom!" shouted Spot.

"Hold tight, Grandma," said
Spot, as Helen bumped her car
into theirs. *Bang!*
"My word," said Grandma, "this is some ride!"
Then Spot bumped Helen's car. "That's the
fun of it," said Spot, laughing. *Bang!*

When the ride finished, Spot and Grandma climbed out of the car.
"That was a bit scary," said Grandma.
"It was," said Spot, "but sometimes it's fun to be a bit scared."

"Where's Grandpa?" asked Grandma. He was nowhere in sight. Suddenly Helen pointed. "I think I can see him. He's carrying something big and pink."

"Where have you been?" said Grandma. "We were worried."
"I got bored waiting so I tried my luck on the coconut shy. I won this for Spot."
"Wow!" said Spot, as he licked the candy-floss Grandpa had bought. "You are clever."

It was time to go.
"Thanks for a lovely fun day," said Spot.
"Thank *you*, Spot," said Grandpa. "We enjoyed it as much as you did."

Sweet Dreams, Spot

It was the start of a busy day.
After breakfast, Spot went with his mum to
do the shopping. There was a long list of
things to get.

"Thank you, Spot,"
said Sally. "I couldn't
have done all this
without your help."

After lunch, he went to the park with his dad.
"Come on, Spot," said Sam. "I'll race you to
the playground."

At the playground, Spot went
on the swings.
"Push me higher, Dad!" said
Spot.

When Spot and his dad got home from the park, Helen, Tom and Steve came over to play hide-and-seek.

Finally, as it was getting dark, Spot's friends went home to bed.
Spot was ready for bed too.

After Spot had had his supper, he went for a last walk in the garden.

A small voice said, "Hello, Spot, have you come out to play?"
"No, I'm going to bed," said Spot.
"Oh well," said the mole, "sleep tight."

As Spot walked by the pond, he heard a frog croak.
"Hello, Spot. It's a lovely evening for a swim."
"Not for me, thanks. I'm off to bed," said Spot.

"Tu-whit, tu-whoo!" hooted the owl.
"Good-night, Owl," said Spot.
"What do you mean *good-night?*" the owl asked. "I've just woken up. I've got lots to do."
"Rather you than me," Spot yawned. "I've had a busy day."

Spot went back indoors.
"Good-night, everyone," he said.
"Have fun!"

Spot kissed his dad. "I've had a lovely
day, Dad. Thanks for taking me to
the park."
"Good-night, Spot," said Sam.

Sally came in to kiss Spot good-night.
"Read me a story, Mum," said Spot.
Sally opened the book and started to read.

Spot snuggled down, cosy and warm. He got sleepier and sleepier. By the time the story was over, Spot was fast asleep.

"What a tired little puppy you were," Sally whispered. "I didn't realize that you were already asleep. I've been reading the story and there was no one listening."

"Oh yes, there was," said a voice.

Sally looked round and there sitting on the window-sill were the owl, the frog and the mole.

"Thanks for the story, Sally," they said. "And sweet dreams, Spot."

Spot opened one eye. "Yes, thanks, Mum," he said. "Good-night, everyone." And he fell fast asleep again.